PUFFIN  KT-434-059

THE SAME OLD STORY
EVERY YEAR

Anne Fine was born and educated in the Midlands and now lives in County Durham. She has written numerous highly acclaimed and prize-winning books for children and adults.

Her novel *The Tulip Touch* won the Whitbread Children's Book of the Year Award. *Goggle-Eyes* won the *Guardian* Children's Fiction Award and the Carnegie Medal, and was adapted for television by the BBC. *Flour Babies* won the Carnegie Medal and the Whitbread Children's Book Award. *Bill's New Frock* won a Smarties Prize, and *Madame Doubtfire* has become a major feature film starring Robin Williams.

Also by Anne Fine

Anne Fine
The Same Old
Story Every Year

Illustrated by Strawberrie Donnelly

PUFFIN BOOKS

PUFFIN BOOKS

Published by the Penguin Group
Penguin Books Ltd, 80 Strand, London WC2R 0RL, England
Penguin Group (USA), Inc., 375 Hudson Street, New York, New York 10014, USA
Penguin Books Australia Ltd, 250 Camberwell Road, Camberwell, Victoria 3124, Australia
Penguin Books Canada Ltd, 10 Alcorn Avenue, Toronto, Ontario, Canada M4V 3B2
Penguin Books India (P) Ltd, 11 Community Centre, Panchsheel Park, New Delhi – 110 017, India
Penguin Group (NZ), cnr Airborne and Rosedale Roads, Albany, Auckland 1310, New Zealand
Penguin Books (South Africa) (Pty) Ltd, 24 Sturdee Avenue, Rosebank 2196, South Africa

Penguin Books Ltd, Registered Offices: 80 Strand, London WC2R 0RL, England

www.penguin.com

First published by Hamish Hamilton 1992
Published in Puffin Books 1994
This edition published 1999
10

Text copyright © Anne Fine, 1992
Illustrations copyright © Strawberrie Donnelly, 1999
All rights reserved

The moral right of the author and illustrator has been asserted

Filmset in Baskerville

Printed in China by Midas Printing Ltd

British Library Cataloguing in Publication Data
A CIP catalogue record for this book is available from the British Library

ISBN 0–141–30275–5

··· Chapter One ···

Mr. J. Kelly

“**N**o, no, no, no, no!”
Maya looked up.
Through the little glass panel in
the classroom door, she could see
Mr Kelly, her new teacher, arguing
with Mrs Brown.

"No, no, no, no, no!" he said
again. "It isn't fair! Last year you

promised me I'd never, *ever* have to do it again!"

Poor Mr Kelly. He sounded so upset. Maya had only been in the school a week, but already she thought he was the nicest, kindest teacher she had ever had. She hated to see him so unhappy. Maya looked round her table to see if anyone else was as worried as she was. But they were all sitting quiet as mice, good as gold, listening and grinning.

"It's the same old story every year," Mr Kelly was telling Mrs Brown now. "You promise me I'll never, *ever* have to do it again. And then, as soon as the weather gets cold, you change your mind."

"Somebody has to do it,"
Mrs Brown said.

Poor Mr Kelly was almost
wailing now.

"But why *me*?"

"Because you're the best," said
Mrs Brown.

At least Mrs Brown knew *that*,
thought Maya. Patting Laura
gently on the arm, she whispered,

"What are they arguing about?"

She said it as quietly as she could, but still everyone round the table heard.

"The Christmas play," said Laura.

"Mr Kelly's class does it every year," said Gurdeep.

"My sister was in it last year," said Fran. "She was a fieldmouse and she had to sing."

"Ben's sister was in it the year before," said Timothy. "She bumped into another angel and fell off the stage, and everyone saw her knickers."

"My cousin was in it once," said Martha. "He couldn't drink

properly with his beard on, so he made a puddle round his chair."

Maya sucked her pencil and thought. Singing fieldmice. Angels. Beards. It sounded good.

"What do you think it will be about this year?"

Everyone stared at her. Then Gurdeep explained.

"It's the same old story every year. Mary and Joseph have to go off to Bethlehem on a donkey, and Mary has a baby."

"It's not a real donkey," explained Laura. "Just two chairs pushed together with a tail and ears."

"It's not a real baby, either," said Fran. "It's plastic."

"It's called The Nativity Play,"
said Timothy.

"Why?"

He made a face at her.

"How should *I* know?"

Maya turned back to peep

through the glass panel at Mr Kelly.
It would be lovely to be in a play.
But Mr Kelly didn't look at all
keen on the idea. He was still
arguing with Mrs Brown, who had
closed the door now, so they
couldn't hear.

"Suppose he won't do it this year?" Maya said.

"Oh, he'll do it," said Laura. "He does it every year."

"But he's arguing."

"He does that every year, too," Gurdeep explained. "You always hear him in the corridors. First he argues that it's not his turn, he did it last year, and the year before, and she promised him he would never, *ever* have to do it again. Then he gives in and does it."

"And it's brilliant."

Maya's eyes shone. To stand on a stage, with everyone watching, and wave your arms about and say your words, loudly, so everyone at the back could hear.

Oh, yes! It would be wonderful!

Mr Kelly came back in, and shut the door behind him.

"I have a surprise for you all," he told them. "This class is going to do the Christmas play!"

Maya looked round.

Oh, no! She'd *never* get a part. They were all brilliant actors. They looked *surprised*.

··· Chapter Two ···

"What's the problem?" said Mr Kelly.

"I can't remember the words," said Eddie the Innkeeper. "I think I know them. I say them over and over. But as soon as Timothy looks at me, they fly out of my head."

"I won't look at you," said

Timothy. "I don't like looking at you anyway."

"Try not to be unpleasant," Mr Kelly told Timothy. "And try not to be silly. If you are Joseph, then you have to ask Eddie the Innkeeper for a room for your wife who is going to have a baby. So you have to look at him or else it's rude."

"He doesn't answer me. That's even ruder."

"That's because the words fly out of my head when you look at me!"

Mr Kelly sank down on the chair with the ears.

"Oh, Eddie!" he sighed. "What are we going to do with you?"

Maya's face burned.

"Let me help!" she burst out. "I'll help Eddie! We'll practise over and over, till he gets it right."

Mr Kelly stood up again.

"You're an angel!" he told her.

"No." Now Maya looked all worried. "I'm not an angel. You said I could be Mary."

Quite a few of them smiled. But only Timothy was mean enough to really laugh at her. Maya was glad to turn her back, and start practising with Eddie.

"Is there any room at your inn, please, Mr Innkeeper?" Maya asked. "We have come a very long way on our donkey. My wife is tired and going to have a baby."

Eddie took a deep breath.

"Alas, I have no room
in my inn," he said loudly and
clearly. "The little town of
Bethlehem is full tonight. But you
could sleep in my nice warm stable
with the ox and the ass and the
fieldmice."

"There!" said Maya. "You know
it!"

"I know I know it," said Eddie.
"I told you. I'm fine until Timothy
looks at me. Then the words fly out
of my head."

"I'll pretend to be Timothy, then," said Maya. Screwing her face up in a frown, she growled at him:

"Is there any room at your stupid old inn?"

Eddie was still laughing when Mr Kelly came up and handed Maya a large pink plastic doll.

"I've found your baby," he told her. "Stuck at the bottom of the cupboard, under the paints."

Then he saw the look on her face.

"What's the matter?"

She wasn't sure what to say. She didn't want to be any trouble. She knew plays were difficult things, and he had a lot to do.

But –

16

"What's the problem?" he asked
again, and leaned down so she
could whisper in his ear.

She had to tell him.

"It's pink," she said. "The baby's
pink."

"Mmmmm . . ." he said, waiting
for a bit more.

So she tried to explain. Spreading her hands, she carried on.

"You see, it's supposed to be *my* baby . . ."

"You can't have a brown one," Eddie interrupted her. "Everyone knows the baby Jesus wasn't brown."

They were all joining in now.

"He would be *quite* brown," said Laura. "He lived in a very hot country."

"He'd probably be about as brown as me," said Ahmed. "And I'm quite brown. But I don't think he would be quite as brown as Maya."

"Does it matter how brown he was?" Mr Kelly asked Maya.

She thought about it very carefully.

"No," she said in the end. "It doesn't matter how *brown* he was. But I'm not sure I'm happy with him being so *pink*. Not if he's supposed to be mine."

And very bravely (because she so, *so* wanted to stand on a stage, with everyone watching, and wave her arms about, and say her words loudly so everyone at the back could hear) Maya added,

"I could stop being Mary if you like . . ."

"Certainly not," said Mr Kelly. "I chose you to be Mary, and Mary you will be."

He picked up the doll.

"It's just a little problem," he said. "You can't put on a play without problems. It's the same old story every year."

He smiled.

"Don't you worry," he told her. "I'll think of something."

··· Chapter Three ···

Mr Kelly looked up from his knitting.

"Stop eating those fruit-gums!" he told the three kings. "Just get on and glue them to your crowns, like I told you."

It was the tenth time he'd had to tell them. Maya peeped at him, sitting bent over his knitting. He was so kind! He never lost his temper, not even with the knitting.

Whatever it was.

He had been knitting away like mad for three days now. He was knitting squares. He knitted them at his desk, and walking about, and even outside in the playground at break-time.

They tried to find out what he
was going to make from all the
squares.

"Please tell us."

"No."

"Just tell us who it's for, then."

"No."

"Why are you knitting the
squares in so many different
colours?"

(He was, too. There were squares
in red and blue and green and pink
and black and purple and silver and
violet and cream and white and

turquoise, and every other colour you've ever seen. Each time he'd finished a square in one colour, he dug in his wool bag, and started off with another.)

"Don't bother to ask," he told them. "It's a secret. Let's just get on with the play."

They got on with the play.

They learned to hum all together so it sounded like the wind in winter.

("Let's have everybody humming this way, please," said Mr Kelly.)

They learned to carry the cardboard trees quickly and quietly across the stage to the exact right places.

("Why is it that we're always

having to wait for the same old trees?" said Mr Kelly.)

They learned to sprinkle soap flakes so they looked like snow and didn't make Anna sneeze.

("I don't understand you, Maria," said Mr Kelly. "I know you're a bright girl, and yet you spend almost all your time being as silly as you can.")

Timothy learned that he wasn't Joseph the car-painter at all. He was Joseph the *carpenter*.

("I don't know why you were given two ears and a brain," Mr Kelly said. "You certainly never bother to use them to pay attention to any of the things you're told.")

Kevin learned to pin up the

beard so he didn't trip over it any more, but the pin didn't show at the front.

("Right. You three just bow to Mary and walk out quietly now," said Mr Kelly. "I said QUIETLY!")

They took the message home to ask if they could bring in their dressing gowns, and any fancy tea-cosies for hats, and all the fluffy white cot blankets or rugs they could find, for the sheep.

("If the rest of you haven't remembered to bring in your

dressing gowns by tomorrow," said Mr Kelly, "I'm going to treat you like babies and send you home with notes pinned to your sleeves!")

They took all the litter out of the piano.

("If I find one more apple core or crisp packet in this piano," said Mr Kelly, "I shall know which class it comes from, shan't I?")

The fieldmice learned to sing their song.

("I can't even *hear* you when I'm standing here at the back," said Mr Kelly. "Now open your mouths and sing it all over again, *louder*.")

Poor Mr Kelly. He was so busy, sorting them all out, and not losing his temper, and getting on with his knitting. Maya couldn't bear to bother him all over again about the bright pink doll.

Oh, what did it matter what colour it was anyway? What did it matter what colour anything or anyone was?

It didn't. What mattered was that the baby doll was there – not lost under the paints at the bottom of the cupboard, but safe on the straw in the manger.

And soon she'd be standing on a stage, with everyone watching, waving her arms about and saying her words, loudly, so everyone at the back could hear.

She couldn't wait.

··· Chapter Four ···

Maya stared at the pile of dolls on Mr Kelly's desk. She felt so happy she almost hugged herself. She'd only been in the school for a short time, but look how many friends she must have already! Almost everyone in the class must have been thinking about her and her little problem this morning when they were getting ready to come in for the Christmas play.

Because almost everyone had brought in a doll, hoping it might be the right one for Maya.

There were all sorts: cloth, plastic, rubber, wood. Even Timothy had brought in one woven out of straw. And they were all sorts of colours. All shades of white and pink. All shades of tan and brown. Brick-red and pale yellow. Why, there was even a green one! ("I know it's a turtle baby," said Eddie. "But it is *sweet*.")

"Take mine," Misao begged. "I know she's a girl, but she has the nicest smile."

"Mine's more cuddly," said
Robert.

"Mine's eyes close properly," said
Laura.

Then they all started. "Take
mine." "Choose mine, please,
Maya." "No, choose mine."

"Choose quick, before Mr Kelly comes."

Oh, no! How could she ever choose? All of them had something right with them. But all of them had something wrong, too. Some were too old. Some were too small. Some were dressed in too fancy costumes. Some –

As usual, it was Mr Kelly who rescued her. He strode in the classroom and the first thing he did was toss something big and bright and knitted and woollen over the room at her.

"There! That's for your baby!"

Maya spread it between her hands to have a look. It was a shawl. A shawl of brightly coloured squares. The squares were red and blue and green and gold and brown and yellow and pink and black and purple and silver and violet and cream and white and turquoise, and every other colour she'd ever seen.

And it was beautiful.

All at once, Maya knew exactly what to do.

As everyone stood round her, watching, she lifted the shawl and spread it over the pile of dolls.

Then she turned herself round on the spot three times, with her eyes shut.

Then she lifted the shawl again,
with just one doll tucked inside.

It might be pink. It might be
brown. It might be yellow or green.
She didn't know. She didn't care.
Wrapped in the shawl, it would be
beautiful.

It would be perfect.

"Thank you," she said to
Mr Kelly, squeezing the doll tight.
"Thank you."

He gave her a big
smile. Then:

"Right!" he said.

He turned to the shepherds.

"Try not to trip over your dressing gowns," he told them.

He turned to the three kings.

"No eating bits off your crowns!"

He turned to the sheep.

"No bumping!"

He turned to the angels.

"No waving at your mums and dads!"

He turned to Timothy.

"No giving poor Eddie that *look*!"

He turned to Eddie.

"Remember," he said. "All the words are safe in that head of yours. Don't worry, and they'll come out right."

He grinned at all of them.

"Right," he said. "Off we go."

Quietly, they all crept down the corridor to the back of the stage. They found their places behind the curtain. Then Mr Kelly pushed Laura out in front.

"Long, long ago . . ." he prompted her.

Laura took a deep breath. She pulled her tinsel crown straight, and spread her giant tinfoil wings, then started loudly and clearly:

"Long, long ago . . ."

Chapter Five

The play was wonderful. None
of the angels fell off the stage
and showed their knickers. The
donkey didn't fall in half. None of
the fruit gums fell out of the kings'
crowns while they were speaking.
The fieldmice sang beautifully. And
when Wayne forgot he was a

shepherd and started machine-
gunning the audience with his
crook, Laura the angel gave him a
quick poke.

And Maya saved the show.

Everyone said so after. She got
off the chairs with the ears and the
tail, and stood beside Timothy as he
knocked at the inn door.

Eddie stepped out.

Timothy said loudly, "Innkeeper!
I am Joseph and this is my wife
Mary who is going to have a baby.
Can you give us a
room for the
night?"

Eddie opened
his mouth to
answer.

Then Timothy gave him the look.

The words flew out of Eddie's head.

All three of them stood staring at one another, on the stage, with everyone watching.

Then Eddie lost his temper.

He reached forward and grabbed Maya by the arm.

"*She* can come in," he said. "She's all right. But *you* can't because I don't like you!"

Maya looked across between the

curtains, to Mr Kelly. What should they do *now*? But he couldn't help her. He'd just put his head in his hands and was staring at the floor and muttering.

So Maya looked at the audience. They were staring too.

Oh, poor Mr Kelly! After he'd worked so hard and for so long! And been the nicest, kindest teacher she'd ever had! And gone to all the trouble of knitting the wonderful shawl, just for her.

She would not let him down.

And she wouldn't let Eddie or Timothy let him down, either.

Maya stepped forward and smiled at the audience – a great big smile.

She reached one hand out to

Timothy, and the other out to Eddie.

"This is a time of Peace!" she declared, waving her arms about and saying the words loudly, so everyone at the back could hear. (They were Laura's angel words, from later in the play. But Laura wouldn't mind her using them first.)

Then she added some words of her own.

"So stop your silly squabbling!"

she told the two of them firmly. "Be friends!"

She turned to Eddie the Innkeeper and gave him a look of her own.

"Innkeeper," she said. "Don't you even have a nice warm stable we can sleep in, with an ox and an ass and some fieldmice?"

"Oh, yes," said Eddie quickly. "I've got one of those."

Then Maya smiled sweetly at Timothy and trod on his foot, hard.

"What do you say, Joseph?"

"Thank you," Timothy said to Eddie, not very loud. Then he saw the foot coming down again. "Thank you very much indeed, Mr Innkeeper."

They all walked together through Eddie's door. Mr Kelly took his head out of his hands, and the play carried on.

And it was *brilliant*.

*

On the way out, after, Maya had to go past Mrs Brown and Mr Kelly.

"That was wonderful!" Mrs Brown was saying. "I know it's just the same old story every year, but every year it almost makes me *cry*: the kings and the shepherds and the angels, and that sweet, sweet song by the fieldmice!"

"I'm not doing it again next year," Mr Kelly warned her.

"Oh, I promise you you'll never, *ever* have to do it again. I promise

I'll find someone else next year. I
know how much work it can be. I
wouldn't have asked you again this
year, but you see, you are the *best*."

Mr Kelly smiled happily. Then
he patted Maya on the head as she
slipped past him.

"Well, of course, I had a lot of
extra help this year," he said, giving
her a big, big wink.

And, all the way home, Maya
felt like an angel.